This book is for

To my favorite person in all of this world,
my mother, Sandra Barnette Lovell.
She taught me to love nature, music, and people
by her positive example. I love you.
—P. L.

Every voice is a rare and beautiful bird,
requiring only that we open the window
once in a while to let it fly.
—D. C.

G. P. PUTNAM'S SONS
An imprint of Penguin Random House LLC, New York

Text copyright © 2020 by Patty Lovell
Illustrations copyright © 2020 by David Catrow

Visit us online at penguinrandomhouse.com

Library of Congress Cataloging-in-Publication Data
Names: Lovell, Patty, 1964– author. | Catrow, David, illustrator.
Title: Speak up, Molly Lou Melon / written by Patty Lovell; illustrated by David Catrow.
Description: New York: G. P. Putnam's Sons, [2020] | Summary: "Molly Lou's mother encouraged her
to speak up when something is wrong, for those who can't, and even when it's hard,
and all of that comes into play when a bully picks on a new kid at school"—Provided by publisher.
Identifiers: LCCN 2019038794 (print) | LCCN 2019038795 (ebook) | ISBN 9780399260025 (hardback)
ISBN 9781984813725 (ebook) | ISBN 9781984813732 (kindle edition)
Subjects: CYAC: Conduct of life—Fiction. | Bullying—Fiction. | Schools—Fiction.
Classification: LCC PZ7.L9575 Sp 2020 (print) | LCC PZ7.L9575 (ebook) | DDC [E]—dc23
LC record available at https://lccn.loc.gov/2019038794
LC ebook record available at https://lccn.loc.gov/2019038795
Manufactured in China by RR Donnelley Asia Printing Solutions Ltd.
ISBN 9780399260025
1 3 5 7 9 10 8 6 4 2

Design by Suki Boynton
Text set in Stempel Schneidler Medium
The art was done in pencil, watercolor, and ink.

SPEAK UP, MOLLY LOU MELON

written by
PATTY LOVELL

illustrated by
DAVID CATROW

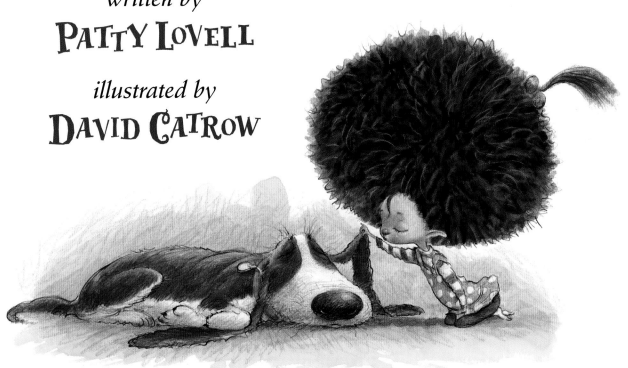

putnam

G. P. PUTNAM'S SONS

Molly Lou Melon was a tiny little girl with a big, deep-down heart.

Her mom always told her, "Be true to yourself."

So she was.

Molly Lou Melon tried to do the right
things in her life. It didn't always work!

Her mom always told her, "Take responsibility
for the things that you do, good or bad."

So she did.

Molly Lou Melon had friends of all shapes,
sizes, opinions, and ideas.

Her mom always told her, "Accept people
for who they are and listen to their ideas,
even if they are different from yours."

So she did.

Molly Lou Melon had a loud voice
and she chatted, jabbered, and gabbed
all the time with her friends.

Her mom always told her, "You have a strong voice. Use it to speak up for anyone who might need your help."

So she did.

In the fall, Molly Lou Melon started school again with a big yellow backpack and a huge toothy smile for all of her friends. She sat with Ronald Durkin and Gertie in the front row of their classroom.

Bettina Bonklehead snickered at them and cooed, "Molly Lou and Ronald, kissy-kissy boyfriend-girlfriend."

Molly Lou Melon stood up and told her, "We are **FRIENDS**!"
Then she exchanged special handshakes with Gertie and Ronald.

"Woodle-woodle, dink-dink, cha-cha, waddle-doo!"

In the winter, Molly Lou Melon had to be
project partners with Bettina Bonklehead.
They "accidentally" painted all over the desks
and not on their papers. (It *was* a little fun!)

When the teacher asked who did it,
Molly Lou Melon said, "Me,"
and had to spend recess
cleaning the desks.

Bettina said nothing
and played a great game
of pirate outside.

Molly Lou Melon was mad at first, but then she played her own thrilling game of swabbing the decks! (. . . Well, desks.)

In the spring, a new boy named Garvin Grape started school. He was small, he wore glasses, and his ears stuck out. He told the class all about Newton's law of gravity in a long speech at the front of the room.

Bettina Bonklehead rolled her eyes, sneered at Garvin, and said, "Big deal," really loudly. Garvin's cheeks turned bright red and he hung his head.

Molly Lou Melon raised her hand and said,
"YES! Gravity is a BIG DEAL!"

Then she scribbled a little note and handed
it to Garvin. It read:

On the first day of summer, Bettina Bonklehead showed up at camp and promptly stuck her foot out, tripping Garvin Grape. He crashed to the ground and his glasses went flying. Bettina grinned and chirped, "Smarty-pants, looks like gravity got ya!"

Molly Lou Melon caught Garvin's glasses in midair, went nose to nose with Bettina, and said, "You must never do anything like that again to my friend! **Friends stand up for one another!**"

Ronald stepped forward and so did Gertie, waving her crutch. They pulled Garvin Grape up, linked arms, and the four friends together shouted,

"WOODLE-WOODLE, DINK-DINK, CHA-CHA, WADDLE-DOO!

If you want to
be a friend, it's all
up to you!"